Maze Puzzle Book for Kids

This book belongs to:

_____

This book is filled with 101 amazing maze puzzles for hours of fun! Puzzles are separated into 3 levels, ranging from easy to challenging. All the solutions are at the end of the book.

This book features:
- 101 AMAZING MAZES
- CUTE IMAGES TO COLOR
- LARGE SIZE PAGES
- SOLUTIONS AT THE END
- PROGRESSING DIFFICULTY LEVELS
- COMPLETION CERTIFICATE AT THE END

For the Parent

Mazes and activities involve hand eye coordination and help improve your kids dexterity and muscle memory through the constant practice of drawing a line through various obstacles. Doing maze activities also helps in nurturing the development of your child's brain, thought processes, problem solving skills, IQ and intelligence by having your child map out the best path to reach the goal in every activity.

Level 1 - Simple Mazes

Let's start with some simple mazes.

Ready? Great - Let's go!

HI TURTLE

4   BIKING

FIREMAN

MR. TURTLE

HUNGRY DOG

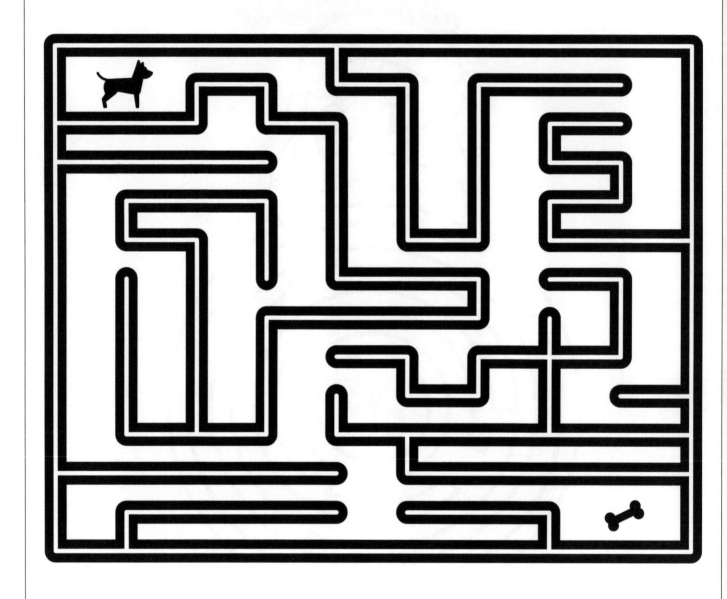

HOT AIR BALLOON

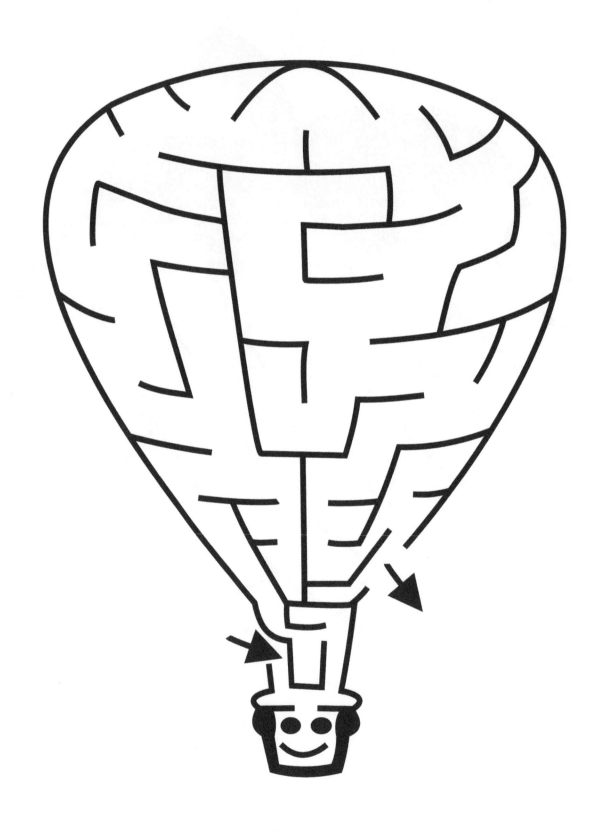

UMBRELLA

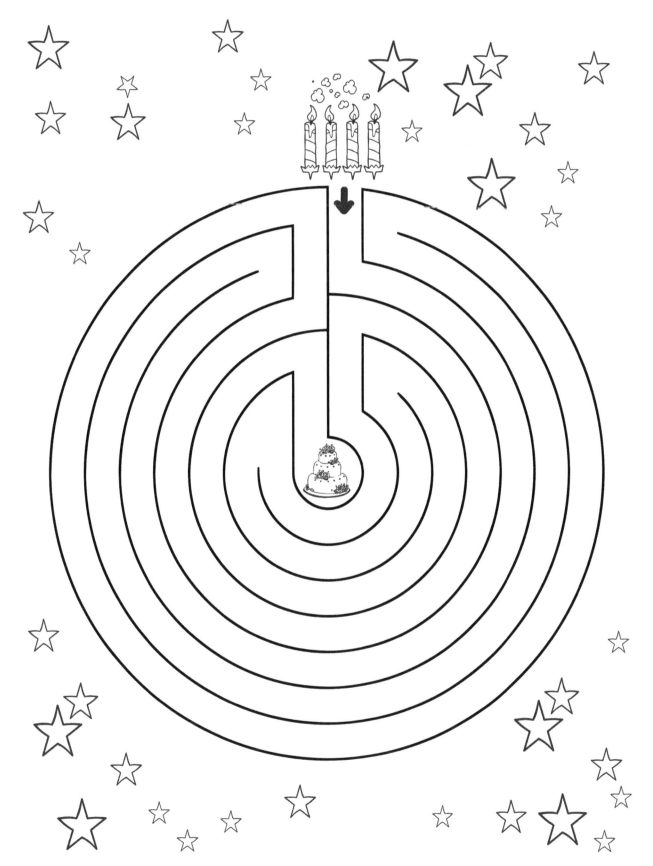

EASTER

TISSUE BOX

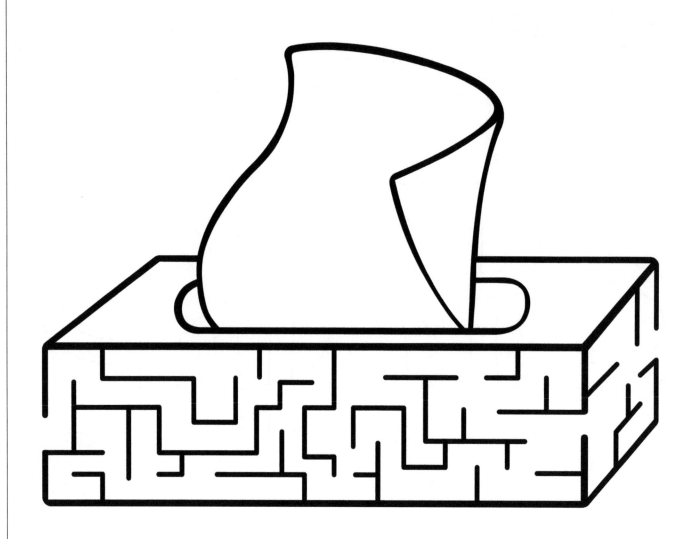

ELEPHANT

LADYBUG

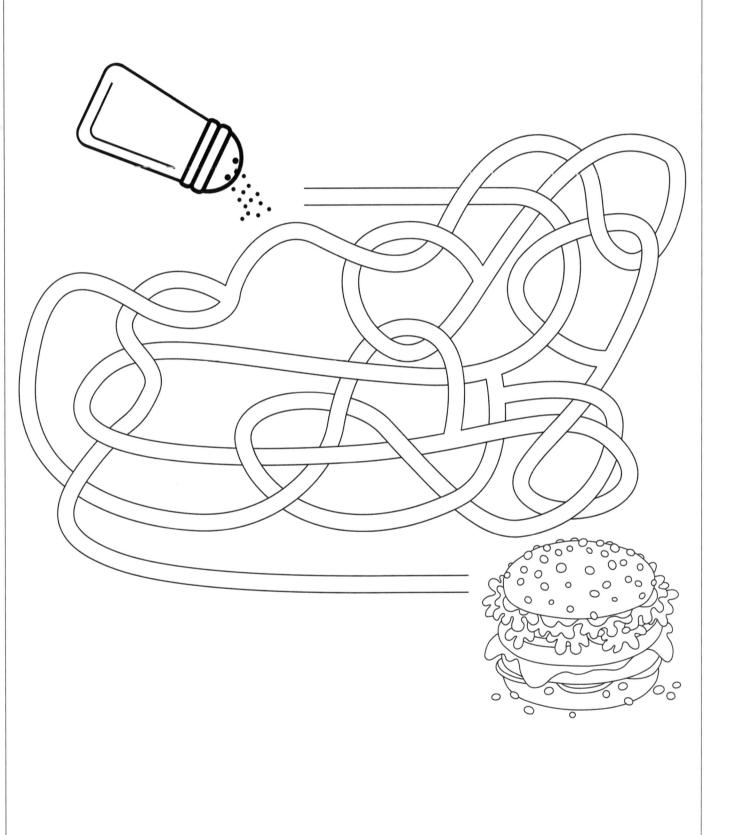

RABBIT

UNLOCK

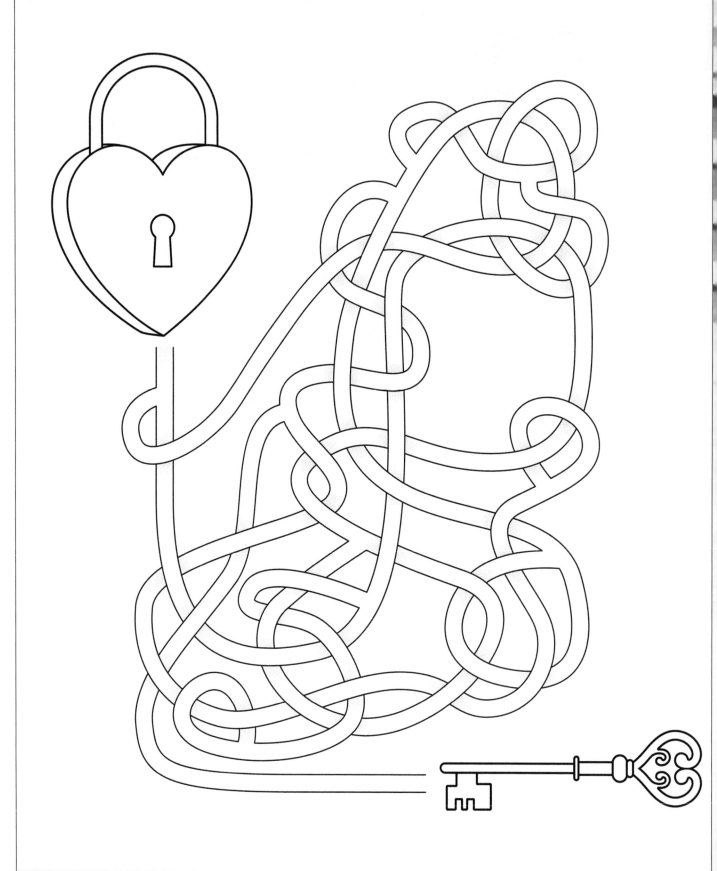

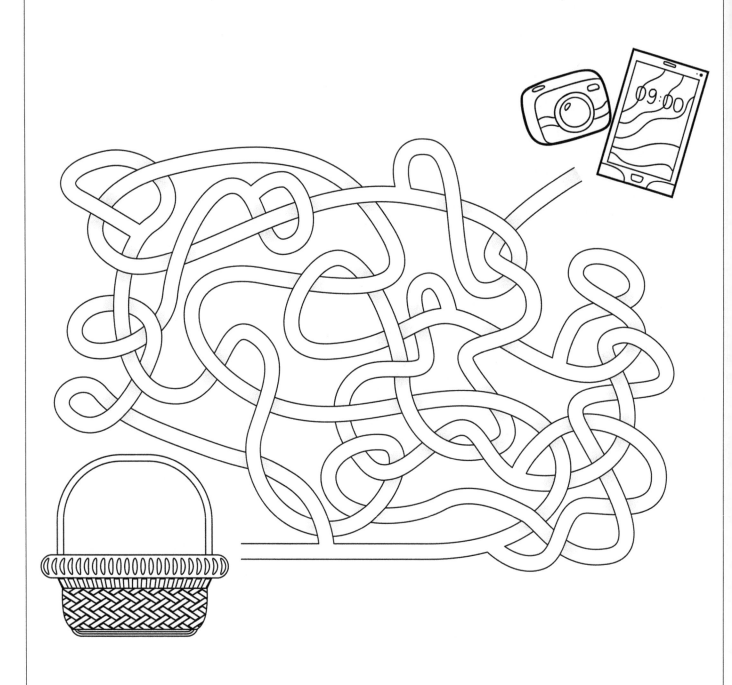

30 WATER THE FLOWER

BASKETBALL

HUNGRY GOLDILOCKS 33

SAFARI

CATERPILLAR

Level 2 - More Advanced Mazes

Great job - You are amazing!

Let's continue and solve some more advanced mazes.

AVOCADO

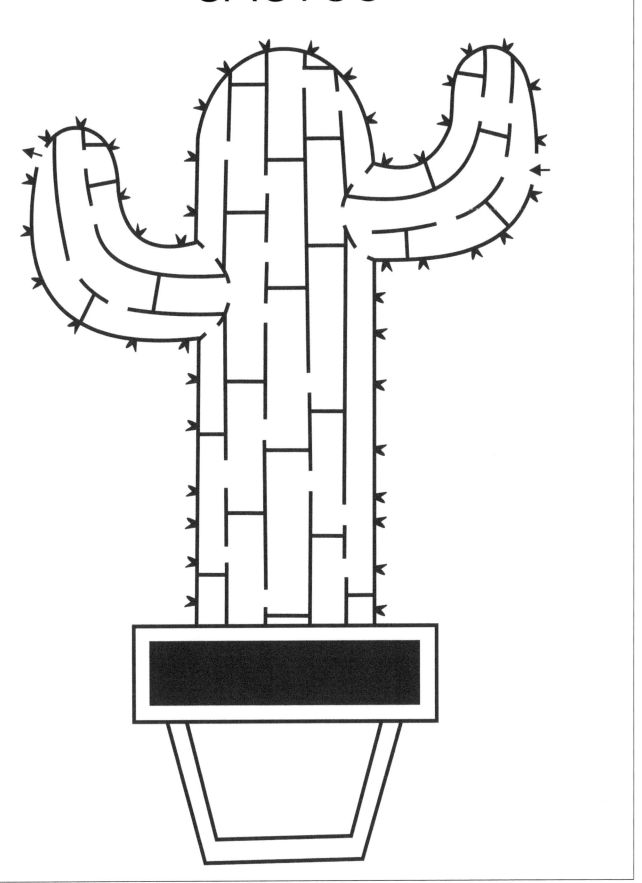

MERMAID

BEE

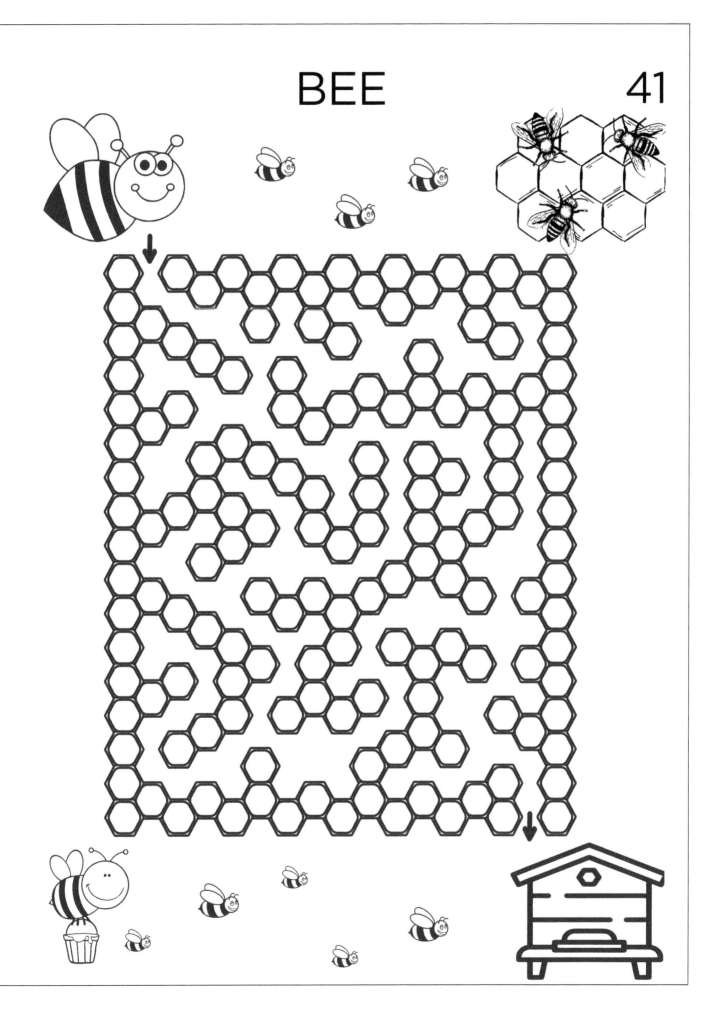

HELLO SNOWMAN

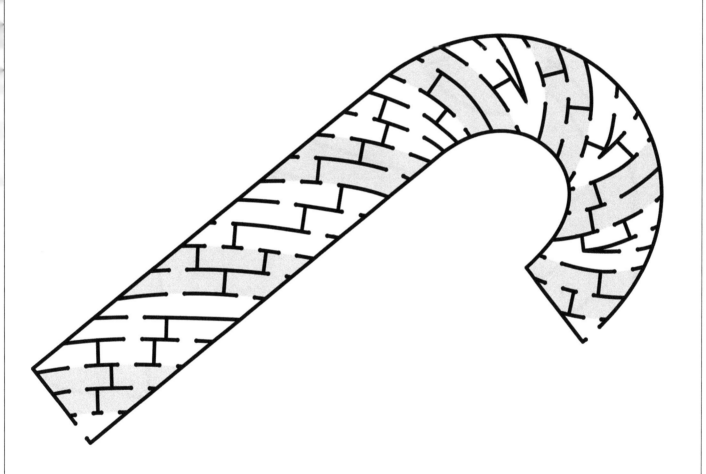

MR. WHALE

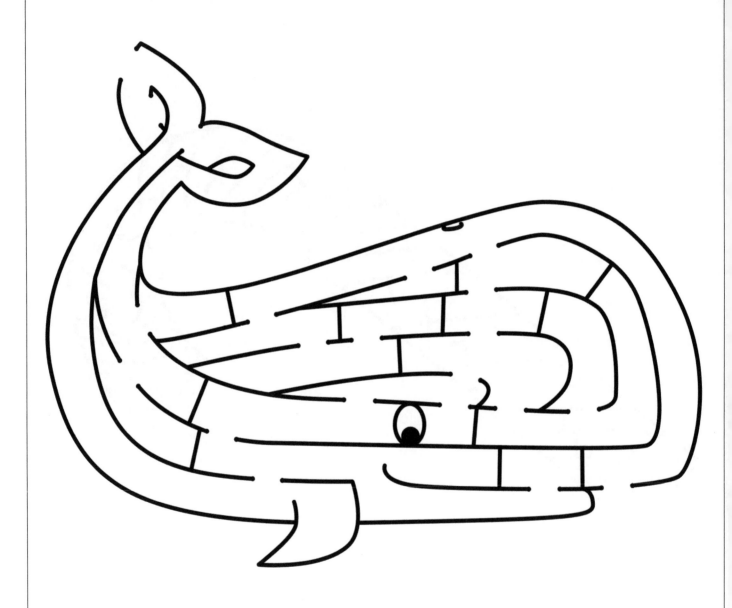

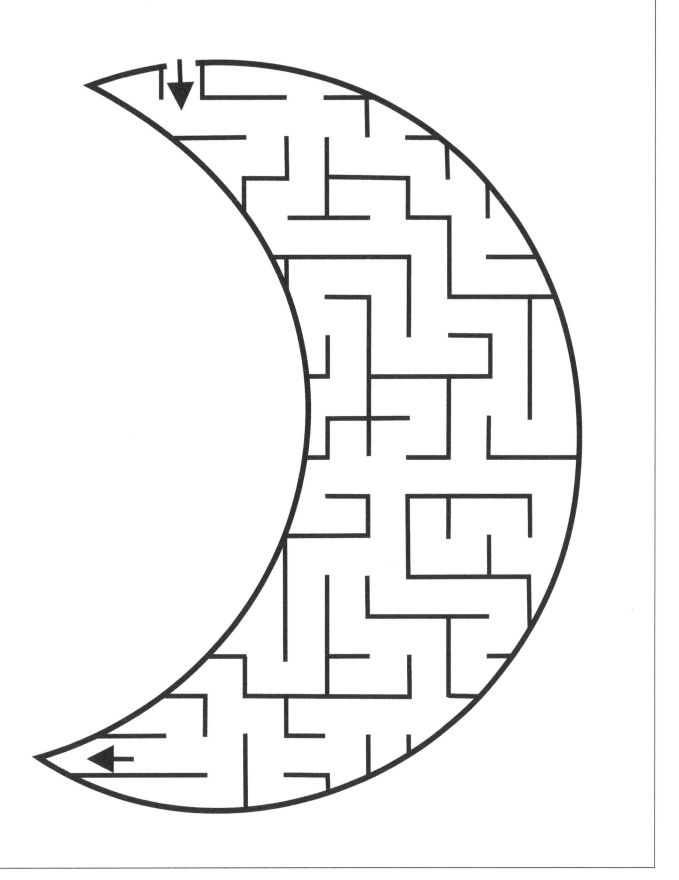

46 HAPPY DOG

HI SNAIL

ROCKET SHIP

FRUITS

TRUCK

LOST CHICKEN

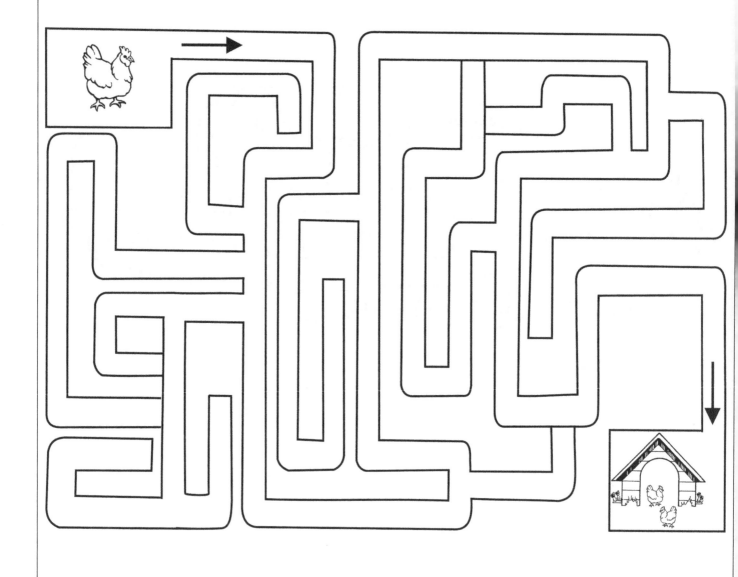

56 GROCERY SHOPPING

DOCTOR

BUSINESS

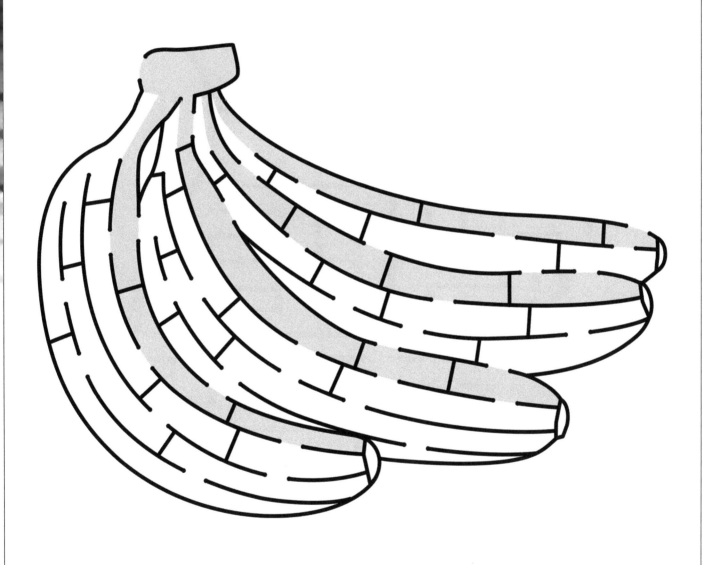

BUS TRIP

GUITAR

66 LOOKING FOR MAMMA

CHRISTMAS

Level 3 - Complex Mazes

Well done! You are really great at this.

This is the last level with the most complicated mazes. Let's see if you can also solve them.
I know you can do it!

SHELTER

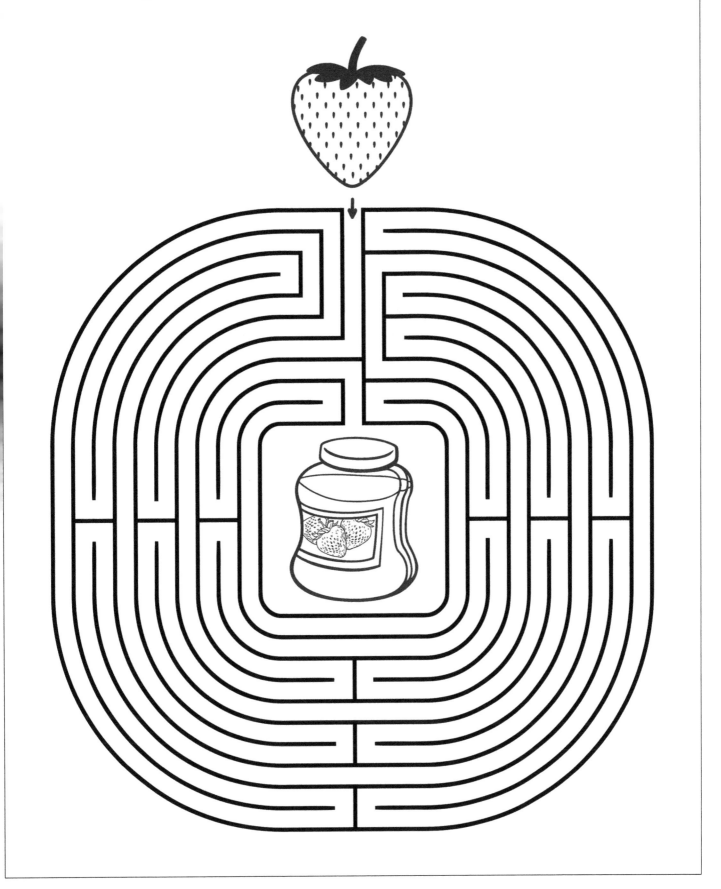

DINING TABLE

COMING HOME

MS. GIRAFFE

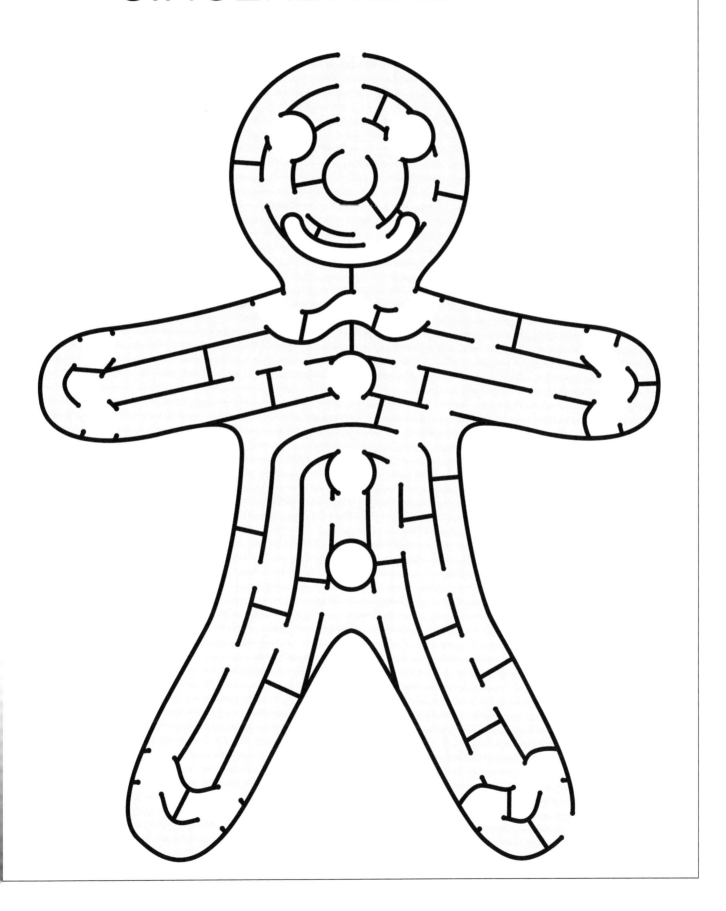

SEAHORSE

PINEAPPLE

SUNDAY THREAT

HELICOPTER

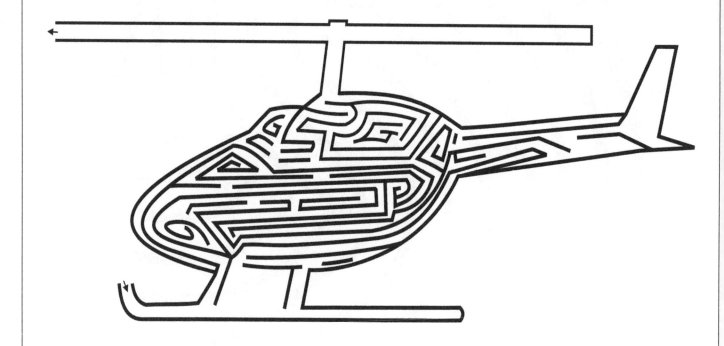

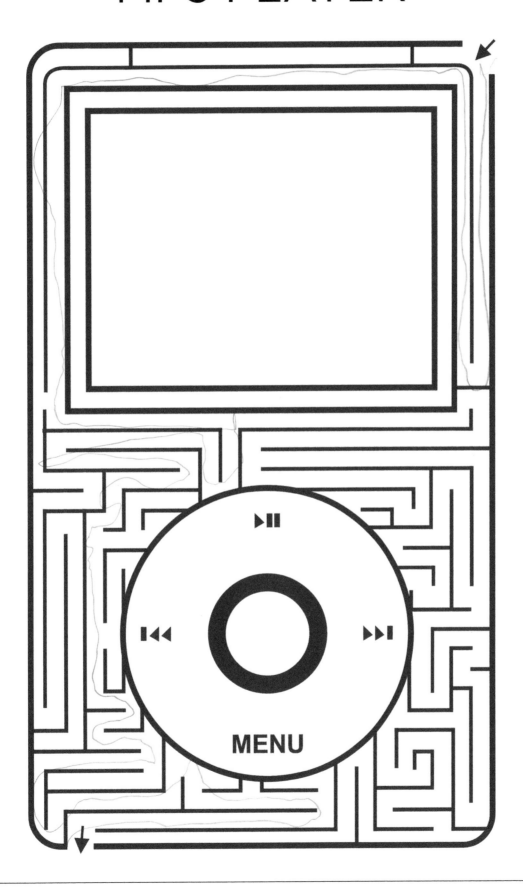

RAIN BOOTS

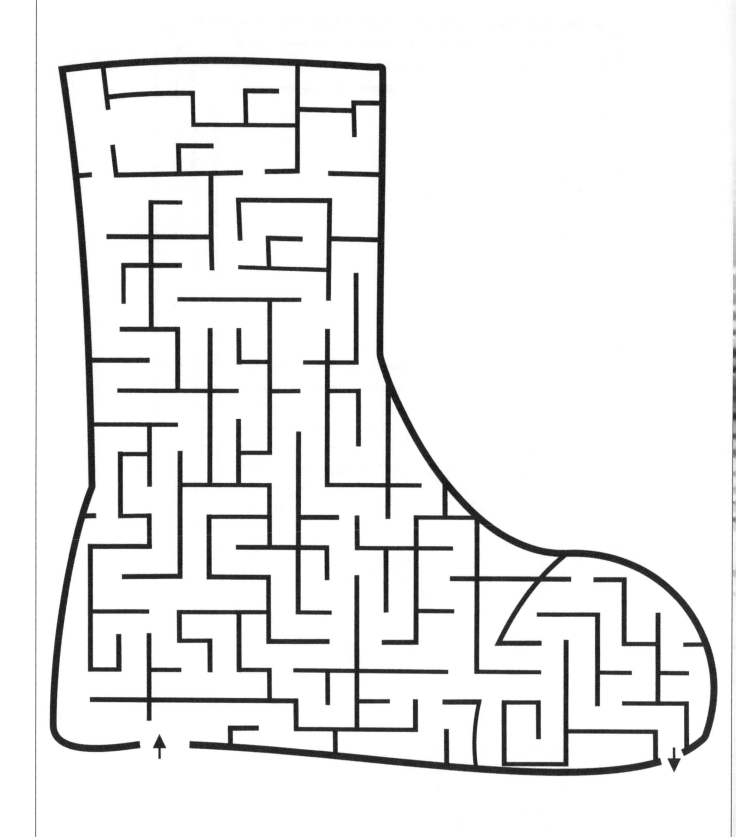

MR. CRAB

WAY HOME

BALL

TEDDY BEAR

FLOWER

BALLOONS

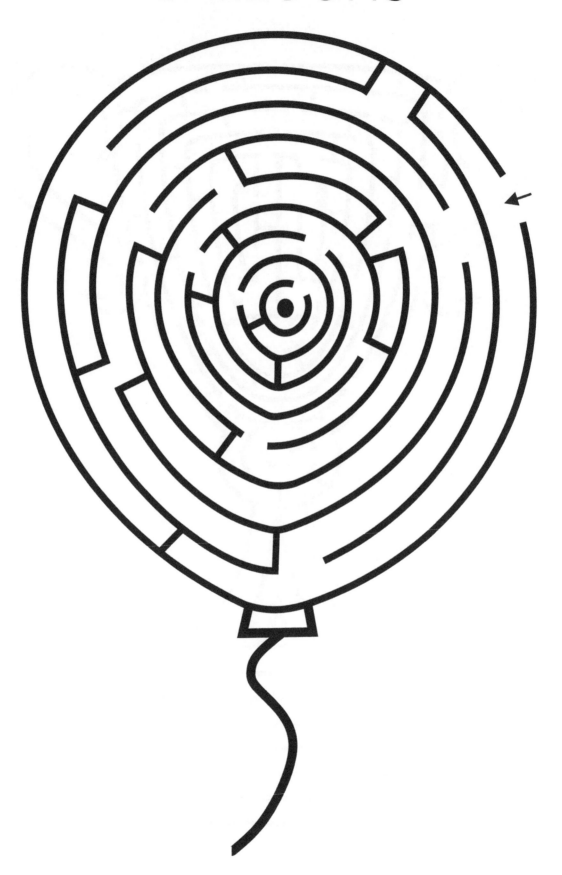

CONGRATULATIONS!

Great job. You rock! If you want to continue with some more mazes, just send me an email to hello.jennifer.trace@gmail.com, I will send you some printable mazes for free.

My name is Jennifer Trace and I hope you enjoyed solving these mazes. I sure enjoyed creating them. If you have any suggestions about how to improve this book, changes to make or how to make it more useful, please let me know.

If you liked this book, would you be so kind and leave me a review on Amazon.

Thank you very much!
Jennifer Trace

- -

Congratulations
Maze Super Star:

THE BEST!

_____

Date:_____   **Signed:_____**

SOLUTION

¹ PLAYTIME

² HI TURTLE

³ LOST SHEEP

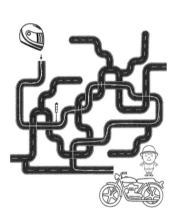

⁴ BIKING

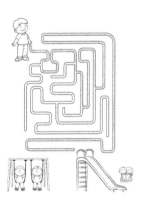

⁵ PLAYGROUND

⁶ FIREMAN

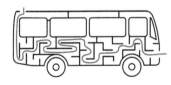

⁷ THE BUS

⁸ MR. TURTLE

⁹ SANTA CLAUS

SOLUTION

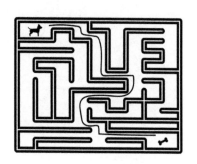

¹⁰ HUNGRY DOG

¹¹ STRAWBERRY

¹² HOT AIR BALLOON

¹³ PIG

¹⁴ UMBRELLA

¹⁵ HAPPY BIRTHDAY

¹⁶ EASTER

¹⁷ PASTA

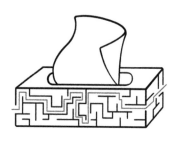

¹⁸ TISSUE BOX

SOLUTION

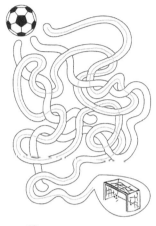

¹⁹ GOAL!

²⁰ ELEPHANT

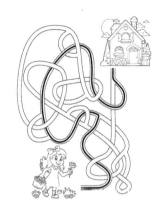

²¹ GOING HOME

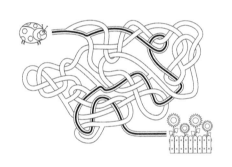

²² LADYBUG

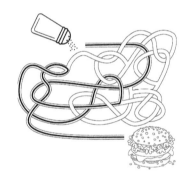

²³ MORE SALT

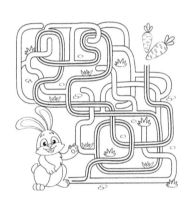

²⁴ RABBIT

²⁵ FRIENDS

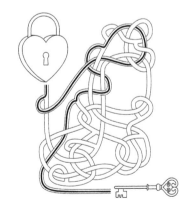

²⁶ UNLOCK

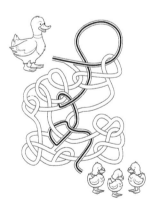

²⁷ TO MOMMY

SOLUTION

²⁸ LOST AND FOUND

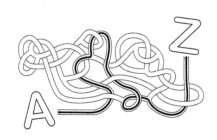

²⁹ ALPHABET

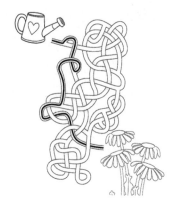

³⁰ WATER THE FLOWER

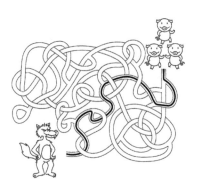

³¹ THREE LITTLE PIGS

³² BASKETBALL

³³ HUNGRY GOLDILOCKS

³⁴ SAFARI

³⁵ OWL

³⁶ CATERPILLAR

SOLUTION

38 AVOCADO

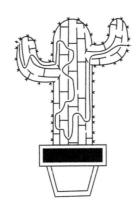

39 CACTUS

40 MERMAID

41 BEE

42 HELLO SNOWMAN

43 THE CANDY CANE

44 MR. WHALE

45 THE MOON

46 HAPPY DOG

SOLUTION

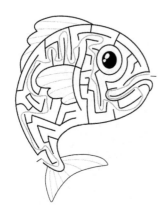

47 UNDER THE WATER

48 HI SNAIL

49 ANGEL

50 ROCKET SHIP

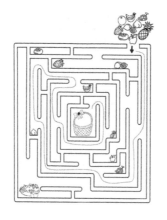

51 FRUITS

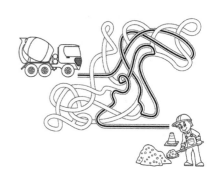

52 TRUCK

53 CROCODILE

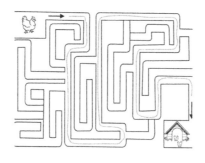

54 LOST CHICKEN

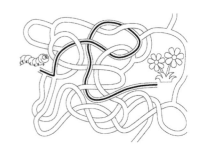

55 CATERPILLAR

SOLUTION

56 GROCERY SHOPPING

57 SNOWMAN

58 DOCTOR

59 APPLE TREE

60 BUSINESS

61 BIG BANANA

62 BUS TRIP

63 FLY HOME

64 GUITAR

SOLUTION

65 FIRETRUCK

66 LOOKING FOR MAMMA

67 MUFFIN MAN

68 CHRISTMAS

70 DAILY CHORES

71 CHRISTMAS TREE

72 SHELTER

73 STRAWBERRY JAM

74 WEEKEND BREAKFAST

SOLUTION

⁷⁵ HAPPY COW

⁷⁶ DINING TABLE

⁷⁷ BIRDS

⁷⁸ COMING HOME

⁷⁹ HALLOWEEN

⁸⁰ MS. GIRAFFE

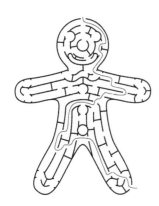

⁸¹ GINGERBREAD MAN

⁸² SEAHORSE

⁸³ RIDING

SOLUTION

84 PINEAPPLE

85 IN SPACE

86 SUNDAY TREAT

87 EASTER EGG

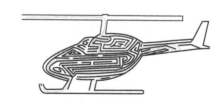

88 HELICOPTER

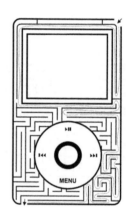

89 MP3 PLAYER

90 RAIN BOOTS

91 SPIDER WEB

92 MR. CRAB

SOLUTION

93 TIGER

94 WAY HOME

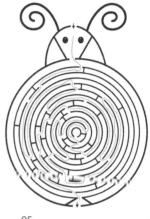

95 BUTTERFLY

96 BALL

97 HOUSE

98 THANKSGIVING

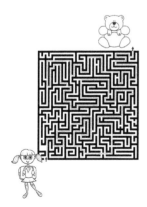

99 TEDDY BEAR

100 FLOWER

101 TROPHY

SOLUTION

102 BALLOONS

103 TUCAN

CPSIA information can be obtained
at www.ICGtesting.com
Printed in the USA
BVHW051334201221
624502BV00007B/257